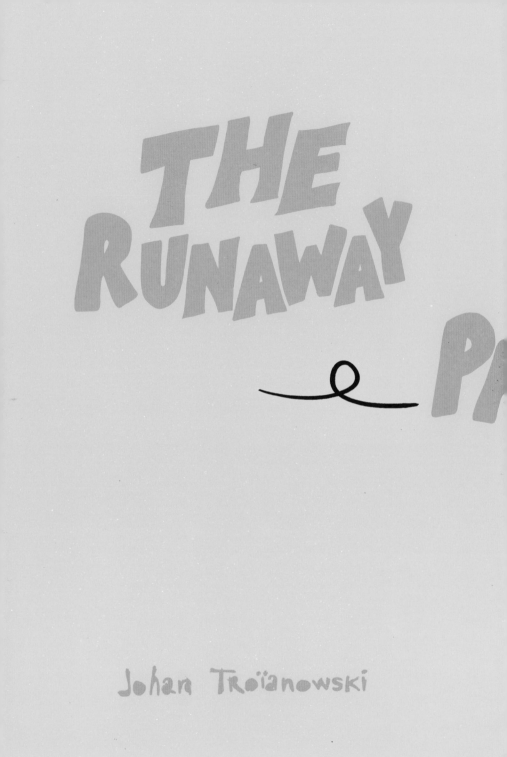

This is a work of fiction. Names, characters, places, and incidents either are the product of the author's imagination or are used fictitiously. Any resemblance to actual persons, living or dead, events, or locales is entirely coincidental.

Translation copyright © 2020 by Makaka Editions
Cover art and interior art copyright © 2015, 2016, 2017, 2020 by Makaka Editions

All rights reserved. Published in the United States by RH Graphic, an imprint of Random House Children's Books, a division of Penguin Random House LLC, New York. The titles in this work were originally published in three separate volumes in France and in the French language by Makaka Editions, Saint-Etienne-de-Fontbellon as *Rouge, Petite Princesse Punk* by Johan Troïanowski in 2015, copyright © 2015 by Makaka Editions; *Rouge et la Sorcière D'Automne* by Johan Troïanowski in 2016, copyright © 2016 by Makaka Editions; and *Rouge L'île des Gribouilleurs* by Johan Troïanowski in 2017, copyright © 2017 by Makaka Editions.

RH Graphic with the book design is a trademark of Penguin Random House LLC.

Visit us on the Web! rhkidsgraphic.com • @RHKidsGraphic

Educators and librarians, for a variety of teaching tools, visit us at RHTeachersLibrarians.com

Library of Congress Cataloging-in-Publication Data
Names: Troïanowski, Johan, author, illustrator. | Smith, Anne Collins, translator. | Smith, Owen (Owen M.), translator. | Troïanowski, Johan. Rouge, petite princesse punk. English. | Troïanowski, Johan. Rouge et la sorcière d'automne. English. | Troïanowski, Johan. Rouge l'île des gribouilleurs. English.
Title: The runaway princess / Johan Troïanowski; translation by Anne and Owen Smith.
Description: New York : RH Graphic, [2020] | Originally published in three separate volumes in French by Makaka Editions, Saint-Etienne-de-Fontbellon, in 2015–2017 under the titles Rouge, petite princesse punk, Rouge et la sorcière d'automne, and Rouge l'île des gribouilleurs.
Identifiers: LCCN 2019018080 | ISBN 978-0-593-11840-5 (trade pbk.) | ISBN 978-0-593-12416-1 (hardcover) | ISBN 978-0-593-11842-9 (ebook) | ISBN 978-0-593-11841-2 (lib. bdg.)
Subjects: LCSH: Graphic novels. | CYAC: Graphic novels. | Princesses—Fiction. | Adventure and adventurers—Fiction. | France—Fiction. | Fairy tales—Fiction.
Classification: LCC PZ7.7.T76 Run 2020 | DDC 741.5/944—dc23

Designed by Patrick Crotty
Translation by Anne and Owen Smith

MANUFACTURED IN CHINA
10 9 8 7 6 5 4 3 2 1
First American Edition

Random House Children's Books supports the First Amendment and celebrates the right to read.

A comic on every bookshelf.

This book was drawn with India ink and a nib pen on 180g a4 sheets of paper, then colored directly with crayon and inks. This edition was lettered with Stanton ICG.

For Mathilde, Lou, Camille, and Pome

THE PRINCESS RUNS AWAY

(AND MAKES SOME FRIENDS)

13

I think I'm lost.

Howdy!

I'm hungry!

Dear reader, Robin needs you. To help her escape the wolf's clutches, close the book, shake it up and down three times, and then turn to the next page.

I'm all shook up!

I'd best scamper before the wolf wakes up . . .

33

Here we are . . .

You're hard to find!

Paul! Isn't this a wonderful carnival?

Where are your brothers?

It's very crowded—and we lost sight of each other looking for you.

47

51

Dear reader, the queen has finally arrived in Noor. But she doesn't know where to go. Would you help her find the carnival? Go to panel 1. Each direction has a number. Pick a direction, and take her to the panel with that number. Keep going until she finds the carnival.

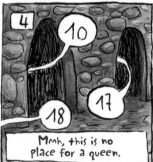

Mmh, this is no place for a queen.

What a lovely view of Noor! Unfortunately, there's no way down.

These characters look shady.

Rats, a dead end!

Hooray! The queen has found the carnival. But where is Robin?

The conditions are perfect.

Launch them as hard as you can, Robin...

...so they can reach the four corners of the kingdom.

What did you feed him?

A seed.

He's going to want more.

BWAAAAA

GROAN!!

Paul, Matt, Lee, and Omar went home and showed their parents
the bag of seeds. Immediately, the boys began to plant a garden
and were soon able to feed the whole family.

TROIANSNOWSKI

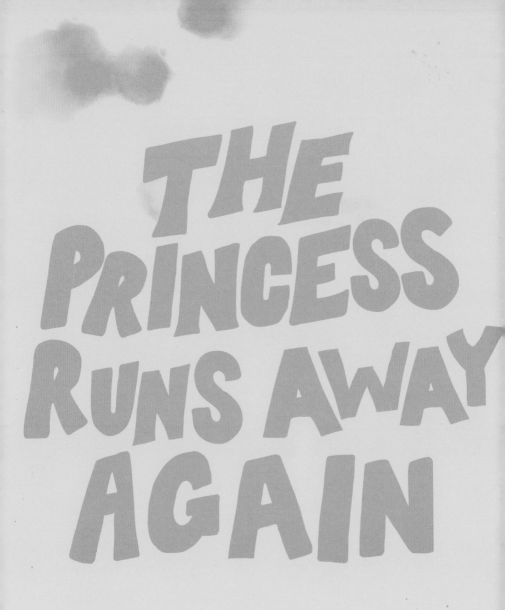

THE PRINCESS RUNS AWAY AGAIN

(BY ACCIDENT THIS TIME)

I've never heard anyone mention this place. It's completely abandoned.

I can't wait to tell the boys!

Robin.

!!

Dear reader, put a thin white piece of paper over this page and connect the dots from 1 to 91. Hint: Many legs!

Uh-oh! I think
I'm . . .

Ow! I've bumped my booty.

Where am I?

It looks like . . .

gold.

Mountains of gold.

155

Hurry! She's getting away!

I must admit— they're clever.

What should we do now?

I have an idea! Grab the columns!

Dear reader, please turn the book so the right side is on top.

Who is she talking to?

Good riddance!

Thank you, dear reader. Would you please turn the book back the way it was?

Um, Robin? My arms are starting to get tired.

TROIA1GNOWSKI

THE PRINCESS

TRIES TO STAY IN ONE PLACE

(BUT THE WEATHER DOESN'T COOPERATE)

Good grief! What do we do now?

Let me think.

Let's walk along the beach. We'll definitely find someone.

I was a scientist in the palace of King Croesus.

He was so obsessed with gold that he even powdered his beard with gold dust.

But he spent his wealth so lavishly that the royal gold mines were soon exhausted.

Since he couldn't unearth any more gold, he decided to manufacture it using the legendary Philosopher's Stone . . .

. . . but none of his scientists or scholars knew the formula for making one!

Like all the other scholars in the kingdom, I searched high and low for the secret of the Stone . . .

BOOM

. . . but without success.

With each failure, the king's wrath grew.

He executed several of my colleagues as an example to the rest of us. So I decided to escape.

Fortunately, I had invented a giant cannon . . .

. . . which enabled me to travel for several days.

It's a time when everyone gathers to share a meal.

They're so big!

Are they the adults?

No! The size of a Doodler is directly related to the length of their hair.

When their hair gets long, they grow.

To grow small again, they simply cut their hair.

Dear reader, have you found the correct island?

240

248

There's no way to escape. He'll devour us for sure.

Relax.

Ahoy there, landlubbers!

?

Another monster!

Robin?

What about you, Professor? If you wish, you can move into the palace and continue your research.

I would be deeply honored, Your Majesty.

Super!

And you, young lady? What would you like to do?

All I want to do is sail the open sea.

Perfect! On my next voyage, you can serve as cabin boy aboard my royal yacht!

Yippee!

Right now, however, we should return to Renoir. Your parents must be worried.

And I'm eager to show your mother my new map, Robin.

Dear reader, now it's time for you to start your own adventure!

TROÏA17NOWSKI

Character sketches

Behind the page! Original sketches

page 113

Page 123

page 128

Page 146

RH GRAPHIC
THE DEBUT LIST

BUG BOYS
By Laura Knetzger

Bugs, friends, the world around us — this book has everything!
Come explore *Bug Boys* for a fun, thoughtful adventure about growing up and being yourself.

Chapter Book

THE RUNAWAY PRINCESS
By Johan Troïanowski

The castle is quiet.
And dull.
And boring.
Escape on a quest for excitement with our runaway princess, Robin!

Middle-Grade

ASTER AND THE ACCIDENTAL MAGIC
By Thom Pico & Karensac

Nothing fun ever happens in the middle of the country . . . except maybe . . . magic?
That's just the beginning of absolutely everything going wrong for Aster.

Middle-Grade

WITCHLIGHT
By Jessi Zabarsky

Lelek doesn't have any friends or family in the world. And then she meets Sanja. Swords, magic, falling in love . . . these characters come together in a journey to heal the wounds of the past.

Young Adult